Hell's Press Presents

ISBN   978-1-7381321-7-1   (paperback)
ISBN   978-1-7381322-6-3   (ebook)

hellspress.com

Fairie Tales

Billy Goats Gruff   Hansel and Gretel

COUNT FATHOM

Dedicated to...

... you, who know how little while we have to stay and once departed may return no more. Fill the cup that clears today of past regrets and future fears. Make the most of what we yet may spend before we too into the dust descend. The moving finger writes, and, having writ, moves on. Nor all your piety nor wit shall lure it back to cancel half a line.

Give me a flagon of red wine, a book of verse, a loaf of bread, and a little idleness. If with such store I might sit by thy dear side in some lonely place, I should deem myself happier than a king in his kingdom.

Rubaiyat. Worth the ducat. Quite an acrobat. If only he would be the model for a diplomat. We could settle any spat. He'd be friends with a rat, or a king or a steward or anybody that could see us how we are, from the peasant to the tsar, who could forgive our predilections both senseless and bizarre.

Inspired by Omar Khayyam

Table of Contents

Preface

Tyranny reigns where we let it. Men are but monsters if permit. Power, you'll see, if you listen to me, obeys an unusual gravity. It concentrates now in the hands of a few, and though it's not solid, it's nothing you touch, the sun it has blotted, as the few they do clutch to the power they hold and abuse. You submit to their ruse. Stitched in a fabric you're knit up in knots, your freedom surrendered to the latest despot. Chained to your place in a prison called nation, the monster on top compels adoration, and if you rebel, I needn't you tell, you'll suffer a freedom castration.

Disobey? This is not something that we can discuss. If you do you'll be branded unfit, treasonous. The wheels of that power will roll over us. If not dead, then your lucky, considered a plus, but you'll not do so again, broken and beaten, a bruised, battered brain, and if you recover they'll open your veins. The power will cower you thus. It's enough to make me cuss.

Billy Goats Gruff

There is much wrong in the world. It is often that when a man dies, the best is said of him, and rarely is this contradicted. But the truth must be faced. Our forefathers, frequently reverenced for their accomplishments, have clearly sacrificed our future for their present. A sorry, selfish lot, our struggles are rooted in their failings. And just who do you think will take responsibility and clean up the mess? You read the news every day, waiting for the second coming, a saviour to relieve you of your burden, and she will never come.

That's rude, of course. You, after all, are a reader, trying to better yourself through knowledge and philosophy. There is hope for you yet. Sadly, your hopes are to be frustrated in the coming pages, for there is little within from which you may profit. Worse yet, you are wasting productive time. When you put the book down, the world will be much as it was when you picked it up.

But don't lose heart! That's just what you're here for. Have a good read, then clean it up. To practice what is so often preached, we must be a century of janitors. Get the place ship shape, raise our kids very well, and the future will be able to take care of itself.

⸻ ⟡ ⸻

There were three, as there so seldom are. All boys, and all named after their father, William Gruff. On the birth certificate, the names were duly recorded William, according to the wishes of the father. The mother was not consulted, and knew to keep her peace in such matters, as goats had not yet established social institutions to protect the meek from the will of the strong. Were she to disagree, the name would remain William, and she would get a good butt in the belly to boot.

One infant William, the youngest, nuzzled greedily his mother's udders, and mother inadvertently bleated a 'bo!'. The two other Williams had, for some reason or other, picked up on this vocal cue, and bleated it on loop as young Bo stood and looked back and forth between them, naked but for the name.

Willam Sr., and the mother too, adopted this moniker, calling his brothers 'the other two' for about a season before deciding they should be distinguished from one another by appellative. The eldest became Bill, and number two settled for Billy.

At a year's end much has changed for the now adolescent goat brothers. If Bo went for mother's udders, he'd get a hoof, and mother would cry. He thought himself too adult for that anyway, and would disdain interest were he offered. Bo was all enthusiasm for goat excursions with his two brothers. They bullied him, but he was resilient. He surfed a wave of optimistic energy, carving hell bent for leather through all emotional currents.

They'd shaved his hindquarters two months ago, and you could still tell. Bo was ashamed, and harboured a simmering resentment, especially towards Billy, as he had done the cutting. Bill encouraged, and Bo's heart was broken. Billy was sorry he had shaved Bo's ass. It was hilarious at the time, but things hadn't felt right between the two of them since then. Billy missed the bond they had shared before the ass shaving. It felt that this fundamental fracture would haunt their relationship to the crypt and beyond.

Billy was introspective and quiet, and the shaving was unusual. Are things like this out of body experiences? Billy felt like another person had done this. Now the bag was at his feet. Billy learned regret was a slow acting poison, and resolved against actions that would sow the seeds in future. He wasn't a coward though. Bill had tried his level best to break Billy to his will. Bill had imprisoned Billy in their pen while he and Bo went on excursions for three weeks in July. Bill wanted to force sole control of decision making for the group. In the end, Billy neither acquiesced to Bill's demands nor acknowledged Bill's supremacy. He was free. Billy did not regret any of his actions but the shaving, and did not begrudge Bill's attempt. The day he was freed, he was as affable and agreeable as a brother could be, unchanged by Bill's coercion.

———— ·•◆•◆•◆•· ————

Whether the fates intervened I know nought, but Bill was built to bop a fat Bob off a cliff one day. There is no question he could do a dog to death were he so inclined. Big Bill bossed his brothers mercilessly, and they responded in kind. They were rough and tumble throughout the land, earning an unfavourable reputation. An order had been issued that Fred the farmer was to keep these ruffian goats tied up to his wagon if he was ever to bring them beyond the confines of his farm.

What could Fred do? He never willingly took the three brothers anywhere. He feared Bill like the devil himself. He had stopped mending fences for some time past, as Bill could barge right through anything but a stone wall. The brothers went where they chose. But they steered clear of inhabited areas anyway, after a warning shot once scathed Bill's left horn.

Click. I've snapped by fingers. And I'll draw your attention away to a village quite remote, by goat excursion standards, which at this very moment you are underestimating. This village is remarkable for its predictability. The harvest was steady year after year, the old were replaced by the young in their duties, the tax collection totals never changed, and there was very little to do for the poor official sent to govern this and many other villages like it all on his lonesome.

Bob, for that is what he is called, was a law graduate from the state college whose can-do attitude impressed a few with party connections and had him on the fast path to this glorious outpost, a bit out of the way. A can-do attitude can be a bit much. Bob was of an entrepreneurial spirit, and didn't sit idly by and let his employment under the government dollar go to waste. One year he decided to enforce an environmental damage clause, written obscurely and interpreted loosely by our enterprising official.

Methane emissions were to be controlled within described limits, and not to greatly fluctuate in value. Bob found a finable offence, and thought that was just fine. He drew up charts and was going to inspect homes for their methane output. Month to month he would record, and fine, against great fluctuation in production. It worked, he fined a few people. Most just paid. The fine was so small that they'd rather pay than tackle this ambitious official head on. All the farmers lied on their taxes anyway, and were occasionally shot subsidies they didn't appeal for or expect from time to time. Bob's minor harassments were operational cost. They called him shit-smeller Bob. Or the Troll, sometimes, too.

Bob wasn't really trying to squeeze anybody. Just to let them know that they were under the watchful supervision of diligent officers of the court. And just because they provided a core value to society while enjoying none of its benefits, they were subject to the full interpretation of the law at all times. He intentionally made the fines nominal. And he recorded and submitted with documentation every cent he collected from the villages he administered. Those back home knew Bob was a rising star.

Among other short term enforcement drives to control undesirable activity, Bob took a post controlling banned substance transfer through his administrative region. Puffed with official pride, and the pro-claimed authority to exercise the law, Bob set up an umbrella and a chair on a solid stone-lock packhorse bridge, one of several trade access points to his purview, intent on col-lecting fare for undeclared substance trans-portation. As it turned out, the heat of the sun was too much for Bob to endure, even with an umbrella, and he accordingly moved his post beneath the bridge, in the shade. He could patrol well enough from here.

He wasn't set still for all that long. Down the crystal path of time clip clopped the billy goats Gruff, sure as drink and the

Irish. The sounds of destiny rang in Bob's ears, to the rhythm of a mini goat parade. That's what the future is, a parade, a current, in which we are thrust along, swept perpetually towards an inevitable destiny - a cold wood box in the earth.

Bob had to shake his head. Those clip clops drove him mad. He scrambled hands and knees up the grassy embankment, soiling himself all over, stumbled at the next to last step and landed flat, belly and face scraping across a lightly gravelled path. Up Bob hopped with a grunt, stood scarecrow, straight-armed an open palm and barked, "Stop! By order of authority!" at these three surprised, suspicious travellers.

The Gruff brothers, for it is they, stopped several steps shy, and there they sat. Bob could not overhear their conversation, but they appeared to behold this impudent

man and his impudent presumptions according to their characters, and not as one.
There is leeway in the goat social behaviour
for much disagreement, and they are forever
butting heads over their differences of opinion. Goats are capable of identifying both as
the individual and the group simultaneously.

After some minutes deliberation, Bo
clip clopped confidently towards the bridge
and the beast.

"Why are your brothers hanging back
there? You go back and tell them to come
forward too. This is an inspection of the
state, administered by the village coopera-
tive, district 13, farmlands equability over-
sight council, who have appointed me acting
deputy vice secretary for zones 17 through
24. I am therefore requesting that you un-
pack all of your belongings, fill out this pro-
visional form stating what they are, and then

I want a detailed explanation including, but not limited to, your last point of departure, your business in this district, how long you might be staying, any contact information for people you know and for your expected residences here, an itinerary of your dealings, and if you could just fill out forms A23B and AB23-D, recording all this information, then I'm sure we can get you on your way before the moon waxes full. Oh, and those horns are restricted trade articles. I can let you pass, but it's a small fine."

Bo took a long look back at his two brothers, watching expectantly from their chosen posts, quite close together. He turned back, and addressed the toll troll innocently, "That's fine by me sir. Baaa. Of course, I'm not the one carrying currency. You'll have to take that up with my brothers. They'll be right along."

"Did those two shave your ass, little fella?"

"Yes, they did sir, the middle one, my brother Billy."

"You run along. Your brothers can deal with this." Bob had a heart, when he thought he could afford it. And now, he knew, he could really show it.

"I'll sit right down on the far side of the bridge, sir, amongst the luscious dewy tall grass, and fill out these forms for my brothers. You can worry about your fine."

Right, good little fellow thought Bob, as Billy belaboured his steps towards the might of officialdom.

"Son, did you shave that boy's ass? Now, you know that's not right. The damage you can do, not just to another person, and that's an enormous weight, but also the harm you can do to yourself. That regret for an action like that can shape you, disfigure you psycholigically, preventing you from experiencing emotional fulfilment. You'll hate each other forever after for representing this failing in one another. Shame on you! I wish I could arrest you right here and throw you in a cell with men of low standards. Now you run along with your brother and think of how you can atone for your actions." Bob sucked and blew a deep, satisfied, sigh of pure erotic bliss.

Billy dragged his relenting hooves clop by clop across the stonework bridge. Billy sat down to watch with his brother, the paperwork starting to blow away in the breeze. And here Billy, not having to say a word through the whole story, departs with nothing but sorrow and shame and the deepest regret. Later in life, when the legend of their story had spread, a fierce quarrel broke out pitting Bill and Bo against Billy, as their tale was being marketed as the Billy Goats Gruff. The proceeds were indeed split evenly, but Bo and Bill weren't as easy to monetize as celebrities. Billy was taking home a bigger portion of the bacon and his brothers wanted in. Greed, as usual, that's what you might think. But there was a deeper issue. Goat society was, in fact, egalitarian for the most part, and maybe Billy's brothers had a point. Bill walked up with the calm self assurance of the physically superior.

"Sir, there's a fine on those horns."

"I'm not paying."

"Then I'm afraid I can't allow you to cross this bridge."

"You weren't here a week ago. I crossed freely."

"I'm here now, enforcing legal code."

"I do not recognize your authority in

this matter. The bridge is free for me to use, and I will use it." Bill is the hero of this story. Bill.

For one painted moment, two brother goats lay in an open slanting field of luscious long grass in the distance, unconcerned as they watched the outcome of an eternally repeating conflict. Tyranny faces off against Freedom in the foreground, in the form of man and goat, before a stone-work bridge crossing a running creek to the land of milk and honey on this occasion. And on this occasion, freedom prevails from sheer strength.

Bill braced his hoofs, lowered the bone battering ram of his skull, skipped forward in a practiced lunge, his entire mass in motion, and crushed flush into Bob's surprised pelvis, lifting him off his feet and propelling Bob airborne over the side off the stonework bridge and out into the middle of the rushing creek, crushing tyranny to death on the rocks below. It took a few more stomps by all three goats, as Bob wasn't quite dead yet. But the goats Gruff managed, for a seemingly rare success by freedom in the modern world.

The gong of fabled lore has sounded for these billy goats. Their triumph over the imposition of the powerful echoes for eternity through these very pages.

The End

Hansel and Gretel

"It's nonsense."

"It might be. We've all heard the stories since we were kids."

"She'd be long dead. Berries will only get you so many years. God knows what she did to get through the winters."

"Well, as you can see.."

It was a cat. It used to be. Splayed out now, on it's back, like a snow angel. But the snow had melted. The fur looked stiff, like an old leather shoe would look if it had spent a wet winter on the path. Not that any of us would dare touch it to confirm.

"Could've been a dog."

We knew it wasn't a dog.

"I'm not staying" , and if the stiff ground protested, it did so in silence as her rapid maddened gait carried her back down the narrow winding trail under her creased white brow.

"That's the right thing to do" , and another disappeared.

"We're alone."

"No we're not." The slanted smile dispersed some of the tension in the air.

"It's just a cat."

They knew it wasn't. Just a cat. She had stooped at the first tufts of fur on the path a few steps before, behind the bend. He had followed the crumbs methodically, but she had stepped around and found it first. He had had an inner panic at her startled shudder, but with will had not let on. They approached together, quite close, touching shoulders, almost cheeks.

The others were gone now. The mystery was theirs alone. They hadn't moved in a minute. Dangerous to have your focus so absorbed. The belly ripped open, the insides gone but for bits of spine. The skin on the face torn too, the skull crushed. Maybe a sturdy boot could crush a cat's face like that.

Finally the spell was broken and they looked around. Like it might still be there.

"This has been here a while. The skin is stiff."

But it didn't help. The eyes were there. They were seen. Watched, even. Their fear was feeding something. Something in the very air. How could it be so still?

"Do we turn back?"

A moment passed.

"Do we turn back?"

"No." But he meant yes. And now her will was equal to his own. She walked on.

He had no choice but to follow.

The trail was a loop. It passed by a lake. They had seen so on the map. The map on the board. At the beginning of the trail. And now the cat was gone behind them. It was a door. They had walked through. And they knew it.

The sky was overcast. But they both noticed it had gotten darker. The bark of the trees, the ridges had a contrast now, veins of black crawling up and down, hiding, what they couldn't tell. And they were everywhere. Like the watching.

Their teeth were touching, tops and bottoms, clenched, foreheads pushing forward. Their steps were fast, but forced. And it went on for a while.

"There's the lake ahead!" A welcome call, said like he'd been saved. They closed the distance in an instant, found a fallen log, and settled down. He feigned a comfort that wasn't felt. She didn't. Her regret was worse than his. She had walked on first. And the door had shut.

They gazed out on the lake, the water still as glass.

"The water's still as glass." , her eyebrows raised, said with joy, and full of hope.

"Glass moves. It's not a solid, it's a liquid."

Her eyebrows fell, her cheeks aswell.

"Let's get going" , and they did.

The steps made little sound, but their attention made them loud. And the watching growing worse with every minute on the path.

"Are we on the path?"

"Yes." But no. They weren't. There was no path. She followed anyway and had no more to say. But then he stopped.

"No."

She looked at him with hate. But what was that above his head? A line of smoke was curling up and disappearing in the cloud.

"Look!" He turned and did. She lead the way again, determined, but for what she couldn't say. The smoke was from a chimney, lost among the trees. It drew up quickly, so it seemed, but when he glanced the lake was gone.

"I"ll just knock upon the door."

"No, don't." But she was gone.

"Come in!" The smile was reassuring, but the gesture left them cold. And worried. And anxious. But now they were in.

An atmosphere, for sure, signifying nothing well. He sat upon the sofa, she wandered over to the fire. Soon a book between her hands was open, but she couldn't read a word. Candles for dim light, and burning wood to keep it warm.

"It's been long since someone's come. I'm lonely all the time."

"We must be going." And they were.

"She must be standing by the fire" thought they both, but didn't share. The light was fading into evening, it was darker than before. Blackbirds hopped among the branches, tree roots slithered through the soil. They walked for half an hour, finding nothing but despair. And it was feeding something hiding, something poison- ing the air.

Again the smoke was curling in the dis- tance, disappearing in the air. They thought they stopped, but didn't, and were once again before the door.

"Come in!"

There they were again, the fire glowing, panic sowing, something growing, and then a thump upon the floor.

She peeled it from her boot, her teeth were showing, it was dead. She shuffled through the room, the tension growing, their reluctance left unsaid. A smile again, a mask, something sinister was fed. The kill was added to the cauldron, boil and bubble, toil and trouble, swinging gently in the flames. An odor, it's sour, an gentle soporific. The effects are horrific. He slumps as he sits on the sofa. The flames flicker fire on her face.

Stir the pot, open a drawer, what are those markings drawn on the floor? Something's not right in this gingerbread house, fairie tale perfect, from a book for a child. Curves and not corners, a nook for a mouse, the air is all soupy, a drug, but just mild. A cat, and she's black, they watch her tail sway. The fire, still it flickers, the setting cliché.

Quiet, now, calm. The mind drifts away.

Gretel awakes, her wet drool on the floor. She rolls herself over, but can't do much more. She props herself up. Just what time isn't sure. Where's Hansel? By gods! In a cage by the door, unconscious but living, judged by his snore.

"Girl!" she hears, but in a fog, imperious, though quiet, harsh and merry, mean and bright. The black robed witch was hunched and grinning, boney fingers reaching Gretel's feet. Gretel shudders, and seizes with fright. "There is the boy!" witch hisses and waves. "There he is now and there he will stay. Die, that boy will if you run away. Cook him, I will, on that very day."

Gretel was free, alone she could choose what to do with that freedom, to put it to use. Our Gretel was torn, she just couldn't decide to flee from the coop or to calmly abide. The lock on the cage was impossibly strong. To try to walk out of the woods is all wrong. They tried that before, but got lost in the haze. They were trapped in the witch's illusory maze. Dreams of escape filled the first few hut days.

Routine settles in, the terror abates. Hansel and Gretel continue debate about the witch and her purpose, her ultimate plan. They knew very little of this boogey-man. The witch came and she went, if she slept they'd not seen. In a rage she would vent, filled with venom and spleen as she'd reach and grab Hansel, stuck in his box. She'd shake his cage madly, and rattle the lock. Then she'd rush out, shut the door with a slam, What's that about? I haven't a damn.

It wasn't so long before the couple
caught on, as Hansel was fed like a pig.
But Gretel would starve three days in a row
before she was offered a fig, half eaten, with
slobber and teeth marks, a hole that a worm
might dig. The witch cooked a stew, day after day, a hanging pot over the flames, with
dead birds and rats that the vultures deign
touch for the burden of a terrible shame.
Hansel, they guess, is due for the stew, a
meal for Nuck's black hearted dame.

Hansel, he whimpers most of the time.
He sleeps when he can, but he's covered in
grime and filth and a stench that pervades.
The whole of the hut smells of death and
decay. He's trapped and he's helpless in the
course that's been laid by a cold, unfathom-
able fate. All he can do from within his cage
is moan and whimper and wait. He's dirty,
unstable, covered in sores, his back, knees

and shoulders do ache. Is it days? Is it hours? How long does he have? Not long till his sanity breaks.

There's many an issue, whether red or dark blue, or it's blue or it's gold, but we're forced to choose. Pick a side, grab an axe and do battle to the death. And all through the fight don't stop for a breath. Keep hammering away with the opinion you hold. Don't shrink from their onslaught. Be stubborn, be bold. Isn't that silly? As if to win is the aim. What is it you win in this childish game? Gather facts, gather evidence, and lay them all out. We'll look them all over with a healthy dose of doubt. We'll struggle with conclusions, and even then we're not done, no opinion ever truly formed, though the proof may weigh a ton. For every time we close that door, we've made a great mistake. "Your work is done, now stake your claim!"

promises the snake. First of all the future holds some cards, you will agree. Calculations we will solve will change how things we see. Moreover, once we have seen fit to banish parity, and into law we do commit a present policy, you have become an oppressor, and create an oppressee.

Commandments etched in solid rock, to lead us for all time? These laws you write are hubris, the fundamental crime. You think you know what's best for us? You'll tell us how to live? Directions for our future men you see fit to give? We are born free! And so we should be. What laws we follow, what rules we make, must be left to us. To Jim and Mark and Mike and Dave, to Lucy, Alice and June, too, if she behaves. To those nearby we must entrust the broad interpretation and administration of laws which they are free to adjust.

Write a constitution, broad in theme, to be a guiding light. Basic principles enshrined, our inalienable rights. And then you must release control, and let the people live. Fulfill the promises of freedom that you so easily give. Let his neighbor judge the man that thinks to do him wrong. It's not for the State to tyrannically dictate that he be punished and for how long. Work out in the community what acts are not ok. Each one will be aptly handled. There may be a stray, but, even under strict controls, that happens anyway. The conditions that will lead to crime must be studied well. Alleviate the strain on man, remove him from his shell and let him shine. He has a bed, the man's been fed, the dignity of law, and watch and see what he makes of he once the hunger thaws. Trust in man to do his part if he's treated with respect. Crime is born of suffering and life long felt neglect. Provide a basic income, food, and medicine when sick. Education, free, accessible, and that should do the trick.

Where were we when we left them? The boy was in the cage. Gretel's mind is split asunder, green stick twisted, splintered. Some days she'd work away at the witches small demands, washing, cooking, cleaning, killing chickens with her hands. Some days weren't so easy, and Gretel would rebel, refuse to do her work, and the witch would beat her well. Some days she'd try to run away, leaving Hansel to his fate. But she'd soon return in circles, the witchy fog would not abate. Is it possible that when we're pushed our character evolves? Gretel one day wakens with an most unshakable resolve. She's determined she will kill that witch, it's high time she should die. What of murder's moral hitch? Please. She deserves it, you know why. The world's better off without her kind. That you will not deny.

The witch is rarely absent more than a day or two. Opportunity there was just to beat her black and blue. But Gretel always found a reason, she would hesitate. The lighting's wrong, the wind is up, and she would have to wait.

The witch, one day, is muttering, a thing she's prone to do. "He must be plenty plump by now. It's time for fatty stew." To the cage she walks. She crouches low and a long arm reaches in. "He's nought but skin and bone, the brat! How is it that he's thin? Not eating what I give you boy? Well I don't care a fig. You'd be going in the stew were your limbs not more than twigs."

Helpless Hansel helped himself, the tricky, cunning boy. He'd kept some bones from supper to serve him as a toy. When the witch grabbed for his arm, Hansel snatched a bone. He let her pinch and yelped in pain, pretending it was his own. Alas! A witch is evil bad, and not a fairie tale. Hansel's ruse just made her mad, the boy was born to fail. She turned away and grabbed a broom, leaving Hansel in his jail.

The witch is hot. She swings at Gretel, just missing with her shot. "Stoke the fire, add some logs, I want the fires of hell be brought! Get up, you scamp, and get to work, you worthless nanny goat. If you don't get that fire roaring, I'll slit your pretty throat."

Gretel's left to tend the fire, the witch prepares the feast. She's chopping onions, carrots too, to accompany the beast. The witch has filled the cauldron with a dozen other things. Iridescent beetles, toad toes, gnats and a sparrow's wing. Scrapings from her fingernails into the pot she flings. A canary from its prison went, when it refused to sing. Thyme and garlic, nettles too, something lucky picked off her shoe, she threw in some star anise, more than a few, and the recipe completed with some ear wax, dug out brand new.

Gretel was sulking down by the fire, staring into nothingness, her situation dire. Arms by sides, her mind it hides, Gretel is forlorn. To die like this, in a witches hut, for this was Gretel born? "Stoke the fire, you damned fool girl!" Witch scampers like a squirrel across the room and grabs the poker from the stand. Cast iron heavy, she prods about, with a stiff, well practiced hand amid the logs, and reveals the coals burning hot beneath. Thinking of the boiling child, a cackling witch bares her rotten teeth.

Gretel feels a surge within, a push to save her mortal skin, an fierce, insistent, ancestral command, an chemical release from some triggered lymph gland. She lunges her shoulder with the whole of her might and knocks the witch headlong, oh, what a sight!, right into coals that are glowing and bright, coals that are snapping with jaws of delight, an miraculous triumph for the good and the right. "Burn, witch! You die!" good Gretel does cry. "Burn the black mage!" Hansel yells from his cage. But where is the key that fits Hansel's lock? It's tucked up somewhere in that witch's black frock!

"Fish out the key from her clothes, Gretel, please! It's been weeks I've been in here. I must stretch my knees!"

"Wait Hansel. You're ruining it. Listen to her scream! Enjoy this, her howls and moans. She fulfills my sweetest dreams."

Gretel walks over and holds Hansel's hand.
Together they allow their relief to expand
and they feel quite merry as the witch burns
to clay, screaming much less now, as the
flesh melts away. Gretel grabs the poker and
stabs the withered witch. She's all but dead
now anyway, and Gretel hardly gets a twitch
from the crumpled dripping mess. Gretel
wears a shining smile, a joy she feels no need
to hide. Murder though it be, Gretel finds
her sense of justice satisfied. She's much
relieved of recent stress.

She fishes out poor Hansel's key from
in the glowing coals. Key in lock, the cage
is open, and out our Hansel rolls. The filth,
the smell, the cuts and bruises, clothes all
full of holes. But he's alright, he's safe as
church, no goblins, sprites or trolls. Wherever life may lead him now, this boy will wear
a smile. Nothing much can happen now to

match this fairie trial.

Gretel's gained immensely from this spot of jeopardy. Wherever she finds trouble, rogues or cads or boors or knaves, they're perched among the treetops, around corners, deep in caves, she'll forever have the confidence to face it with resolve. In crisis some will panic, but our heroes will evolve. We meet now for the first time our new Gretel, since reborn. Give this flower space to live, and beware, for she's grown thorns.

The End

Acknowledgments

This is bad, and that's not good. This doesn't work the way it should. I'd change it all if I only could. But let's be honest, it's understood, you'd screw it up, you surely would. Your blind unquestioned hubris is a bold faced falsehood.

So what to do? Where's the fix? What have we in our bag of tricks? What tools do we have to throw into the mix? Some will point to politics. They hope legal addendum that they affix will stop the steady flow of the river Styx. Some will reach out for their crucifix. But problems won't be solved with a couple of sticks.

The children, they aren't ruined. They still have a chance. It seems a bit impertinent at first glance. What do children know of national finance? They wet the bed, and they pee their pants. They run in circles all day long in a narrow freelance dance. But here now I look towards you with reasonable askance: could it be any worse than our present, which is cursed? We've done no better fixing things while mired in a miserable political trance?

Help them, teach them, raise them well. Funding, resources, a life outside a cell that we now call a school, where so many turn out fools, wet from head to toe from their messy day long drool. Double and triple and ever so much more as a percent of GDP into the children we should pour. For their generation we should be a guarantor.

Fill them with the knowledge of all that's come before. Identify the capable and give them all we can. Help them grow up well and form a master plan. Listen to them, guide them. Within a single lifespan, let them take the future from the hands of the madmen. We have made a mess, now it's time to clean it up. To do that all ourselves would be silly and abrupt.

Author

March! An hour at a time, as though escaping from a crime. The crime your birth, and since that day you've wasted all the hours away. And what will happen? Soon you'll die. A fact you surely won't deny. How, then, can you leave your mark within a world so filled with dark?

Chances there are all around. A king you'll be, without a crown, if with the children you will play. Fairie tales, a cart, a sleigh, draughts or chess, a ball you throw, perhaps a game of tic tac toe. Through children is the whole world lit. To them alone will Nuck submit.

From State we've had our children taught. Obedience is what they've sought. To raise us as a race of slaves, to punish when we misbehave. But this is not just what we want. Our souls are shriveled, starved and gaunt. Emerging from our State run cult, not one of us has grown adult.

Adult is freedom, pure and plain. But freedom that's been yoked with reins. Principles we hold to fast. Morals forged, in iron cast. Rules we write, we choose ourselves, an order to our moral shelves. Not imposed from high above, not inflicted with a shove, but chosen carefully, out of love.

Some may say most men are bad, so straighten out the little lad. We'll clean him up and and make him work, one day he'll serve as the perfect clerk. I say the chains on him we place will send the honest child berserk.

Listen, then, to what he thinks. He's out of line? Don't make a stink. Don't train him from your hand to shrink. From your hand he should expect a patient, measured, true respect. This can produce the desired affect. Treat well the future's architect.

Hell's Press

In prison does a man reside, and ain't it just his luck? To cheat and lie and steal and more to earn a measly buck. "They need me!" thinks he. "I can help! Don't shove me in the muck. I am, indeed, a moral man, but somehow you suck me down into the gutter, mired in filth I daren't utter, would I try I'd only stutter, hear me swear now, ...